CRAZY LIKE ME

CRAZY LIKE ME

Memories & Musings of a Retired Small Town Doctor

A Novel

Jerome A. Kessler, M.D.

iUniverse, Inc.
New York Lincoln Shanghai

CRAZY LIKE ME
Memories & Musings of a Retired Small Town Doctor

Copyright © 2007 by Jerome A. Kessler, M.D.

iUniverse books may be ordered through booksellers or by contacting:

iUniverse
2021 Pine Lake Road, Suite 100
Lincoln, NE 68512
www.iuniverse.com
1-800-Authors (1-800-288-4677)

This is a work of fiction. All of the characters, names, incidents, organizations, and dialogue in this novel are either the products of the author's imagination or are used fictitiously.

The drawings in this book (the front cover and page 77) are by the author's middle son, Joel A. Kessler.

ISBN-13: 978-0-595-42398-9 (pbk)
ISBN-13: 978-0-595-86735-6 (ebk)
ISBN-10: 0-595-42398-1 (pbk)
ISBN-10: 0-595-86735-9 (ebk)

Printed in the United States of America

Contents

1. Beginning Thoughts

Driving to his new job, John Smith asks himself: "What did I forget?" He does his daily checklist: "Shovel, rake, hoe—check. Chainsaw, mower, edger—got 'em. Hedge shears, rope, ladder, tree saw—got those too." He grins with the thought: He has everything he could ever want … In truth, he does have everything he needs—for the day's landscaping work, as well as for the other challenges he might face today.

So many times John has started on his way, paused to reflect on where he's been, and been struck by the vague feeling that there is something left behind. Sometimes he quickly remembers what he forgot, picks it up, and heads on his way. Other times he goes on his way, feeling uneasy about what is missing, and mulls along until the deficit becomes clear.

"Gasoline!" John tells himself. "How did I expect to run the chainsaw without gasoline?" Smith berates himself for the mistake. Now he has to drive all the way home to pick up the gas can. He wants to be as efficient as possible. Oversights can cost time and money. Today he has to drive few miles out of his way, so *it's no big deal*. But he lets it bother him way more than it should. If he was the president of the USA, CEO of a company, or a doctor—then those minor mistakes might matter. But today John Smith is just a landscaper. Even those people (with important jobs) forget things. Do they worry about their mistakes? Everyone forgets things. When people in authority mess up, it can have a snowballing effect; and the consequences can be significant.

John Smith is a worrier. He sweats the details. He always has been. As a boy, he worried about how he looked, how he was doing, and what people thought of him. As a young man, he worried that he might not find a suitable wife. He worried about his education. And he worried about how he would turn out. Smith wanted to have a good job, make a lot of money, and have the respect of the community. In his last job, Smith worried about the people he was trying to help; and he got upset if everyone wasn't trying as hard as he was.

John's mother always told him: "Try hard!" His father always told him: "Take it easy." Somehow he translated these parental messages into "Try hard, but don't screw up!" And, naturally enough, he grew up trying hard—but afraid of messing up.

Childhood has a lot of mixed messages like that. It's nobody's fault—it's just the way it is. Our society also teaches us the importance of *winning*. It's okay to want to win. If you don't, then chances are you just don't care. Apathy doesn't solve anything. And so Smith learned to try hard, give it his best, work, make himself better, and work some more. He wanted to become somebody important. And he tried not to let any obstacles deter him from reaching his goals. Smith didn't let anything or anyone get in his way.

When he was a kid, there was a bully in John's neighborhood. The bully pushed John and other kids around. During one of these scuffles, John's grandmother tried to protect him from this bully. It was one of the most embarrassing episodes of John's life. The boys teased John about that for a long time. The ridicule stopped when John later stood up to the bully, and gave him two black eyes in the process.

Only crazy people like getting pushed around. Some people run from difficulties, and others attract them like a magnet. It isn't clear whether this is by nature or nurture, but John seemed to attract problems. He was never afraid of a challenge. He felt the need to prove himself. He seemed to enjoy adversity. All too often he found himself in "win or lose" scenarios—rather than "win-win" situations that psychologists prefer.

The things we learn in childhood stay with us in adulthood. Wanting to win and be successful is natural enough, but the external world doesn't always cooperate. And if we don't adjust we are regarded as unyielding, stupid, or crazy.

It is inevitable that a person receives some criticism in their lifetime. A lot of it shouldn't be taken seriously. For example, as a kid John was teased about being from a poor family. Up until that time, he didn't think of himself as poor. He thought it was cool that he helped his dad do janitorial work. Cleaning toilets wasn't that bad. Running the buffer to wax floors at the school was fun. But kids started to tease him about being "the janitor's kid." He started to notice that his dad had calloused hands and didn't shave too well. John's dad was actually a Mailman in the daytime, but did a variety of part-time jobs each evening. John started to realize that his dad worked all these jobs out of financial necessity—and not just for the fun of it.

John always had to help with his dad's part-time jobs. As time went on, he resented having to help his dad, especially when the other kids were playing baseball. But now his dad is gone ... John's dad died of a heart attack when he was just 49 years old. John was only 13. John felt bad that he hadn't helped his dad even more. He even felt responsible for his dad's death.

John's dad was landscaping the local doctor's clinic when he had his fatal heart attack. He had just seen that same doctor about chest pain, and Dr. Weeds made a tragic misdiagnosis. (All names and events in this book are, of course, fictional.) Doctor Weeds told John's dad that his chest pain was "indigestion." This medical mistake denied John's father the care he needed.

Dr. Weeds was a brusque and condescending General Practitioner. He seemed to be mad at the world. He certainly didn't seem to care much for his patients. A few years earlier, Dr. Weeds had a son who was run over while riding his bicycle. Losing his son no doubt soured his outlook toward life. With the indifference he had, Dr. Weeds should have quit medicine. His tragedy resulted in countless other tragedies of misdiagnosis and poor medical care.

When John's dad died, it left a wife and eight kids wondering how they would ever manage. Everybody cried at the funeral. John cried, too; but he was also mad. John vowed that he would somehow *right the wrong* that had been done. John told everyone that he would someday become a doctor. In his teenage brain, John might have thought he could magically undo his father's death.

John Smith did eventually become a doctor. After high school, it took an additional 14 years to complete his education (college, medical school, and residencies). He received certification in the fields of Internal Medicine, Family Practice, and Geriatrics. He learned a lot of medicine, and also learned a few things about life. John eventually came to realize that it was cigarette smoking that caused his father's fatal heart attack. And he realized he couldn't bring his dad back from the grave.

Doctor John Smith never forgot how his dad died. He often saw his dad (and other family members) in the patients he cared for. He learned that doctors can't always make things right. Even if doctors were perfect—and they're not—people would still get sick, suffer heart attacks, get cancers, and experience tragedy. A caring and competent doctor can make a difference, though. Sometimes an accurate diagnosis and intervention can prevent suffering and postpone death. Skillful surgery and appropriate medication can provide almost miraculous benefit to a patient and their loved ones. But people get sick again, he learned; and the next problem might be harder to treat.

A doctor's life is full of many rewards and also many disappointments. Some doctors make a great deal of money. Unless they are big city super-specialists, though, doctors don't make as much as people think. They'd make more money if they had gone into another profession. Doctors generally do get a fair amount of public respect. Some people resent doctors, however. The "MD" label still gives doctors a variety of benefits, which they don't always appreciate …

Policemen shake their heads at doctors who drive too fast. Doctors don't get their fair share of speeding tickets. Doctors who habitually speed feel they are entitled to do so because of their occupation; and this usually has nothing to do with patient care.

It's hard to give up the rewards of a doctor's life—but that's exactly what John did a few years ago. John's doctor told him to take an early retirement. The stress wasn't worth it anymore. The job had become hazardous to his health. He is now learning how to get on with his life. He enjoys non-doctor activities. Today he is a landscaper. Sometimes he pictures himself as an author. He also has been a busboy, coach, cook, father, fix-it man, husband, janitor, librarian, painter, paperboy, salesman, teacher, and truck driver.

Doctor John had close contact with people facing a variety of challenges. The trust and esteem that a patient gives a doctor is not something that should be taken for granted. As a doctor, he always wanted to make the right diagnosis and prescribe the right treatment. The *science* of medicine is obviously important, and is openly discussed in the media. The *art* of the medicine is often neglected. The doctor-patient relationship may be more important than whatever pills and surgery you receive.

Doctors should appreciate the unique relationship they have with their patients. Doctors can learn as much from their patients as patients learn from their doctors. In that light, John appreciates the many things that his former patients taught him. Over the years, patients shared their hopes, dreams, fears, and frustrations with Doctor John.

"Enough talk about the past," John says to himself. "I've got a job to do … Someday I'll write a book about these things," he muses. But for now he must put aside his thoughts about the past, and start the day's landscaping job. "I like digging holes," he tells himself, and others. People think it's strange: a medical doctor who digs holes for a living. "Maybe they feel sorry for me," he thinks. And others wonder what he's really up to. Dr. Smith tells people he's writing a book. That strikes people as a more honorable thing to do. The truth is, perhaps, that John is writing a book so that he can better justify his landscaping.

Kessler Wedding—October 26, 1946

"Love ... never gives up."

Bible, I Corinthians 13:7, NIRV

2. Dad

Teachers and historians politely discuss the causes of World War II. It was a time when the evils of totalitarianism arose from the global economic depression of the 1930s. Germany, Italy, and Japan were anxious to improve their status in the world. These countries banded together as the Axis alliance. They all hoped to correct perceived injustice they had received following recent geopolitical losses.

Experts ask: "Would there have been world war if not for Hitler?" and "Would the United States have entered the war if Japan hadn't bombed Pearl Harbor?"

These are important historical questions. My dad might have given these ideas some thought. More likely than not, though, he went to war for the simple reason that all his friends were signing up; and he wanted to do the right thing. A teacher's son, Dad was a good student at a prestigious college. He was promised officers training when he enlisted. The army filled their quota for officers when they got to "H" in the alphabet, however; so Dad was put in the infantry.

My name is John Smith; and I learned this (and other interesting information) about my dad when I found a shoebox of his letters in the attic. Studying his correspondence home captured my interest like no other subject. It is an age-old belief that a young man should know his father in order to better know himself; and I believe that truth also applies to me.

As Dad crossed the Atlantic Ocean in 1943, he thanked God for taking care of him and his fellow soldiers. He expressed great faith that the U.S. would not only win the war, but would also take care of its soldiers. And after arriving in Northern Africa, he admired the beauty of the land. He was curious about the culture of the Arab people, and couldn't believe that their leaders lived in ridiculous luxury while the masses lived in utter poverty. His letters never were allowed to say exactly where he was, or what his mission might be; but he never forgot to thank God and pray that he be protected from danger.

Dad's first combat experience was in January of 1944. It was not the grand and glorious experience he might have hoped for, however. His company was supposed to cross the ice-cold waters of the Rapido River in central Italy, secure a foothold, and fight the enemy. German soldiers were entrenched across the river, where they were hiding in and around the monastery of Mount Cassino. The German forces were almost insurmountable from this vantage point. Asking the Americans to dislodge this force was truly an impossible mission. It was a suicide campaign. The newspapers of the day reported that approximately 2000 Americans (of the 34th and 36th Divisions) were killed or captured that day. Only 17 of Dad's company of 184 men (the 143rd Regimental Combat Team) survived.

The newspapers said "these men did not die in vain." The attempted crossing of the Rapido River had been done to divert the enemy's attention away from the nearby campaign at Anzio beachhead. The men in Dad's company were apparently considered expendable. The main attack was led by Major General John Dahlquist, and his troops were able to advance 300 miles during the next month. This eventually allowed Allied forces to recapture Rome. Rather than complain about being used in a decoy mission, Dad—in his inimitable way—thanked God that he "was one of the fortunate few" of his company to have survived the experience.

Dad suffered a shrapnel injury to his neck in that battle. He suffered physical pain and neck spasms from this injury for the rest of his life. He was captured by the Germans, and spent the next 30 months of his life in a German P.O.W. camp. Although he lost 50 pounds during that time, his postcards of the day express gratitude for the care he received from the Germans. Dad, who knew how to speak German, organized a program of athletics in his camp, and received an award from the YMCA for this activity.

Mom says Dad had many girlfriends before he left for the war. She was somewhat surprised that his letters started calling her "my gal." As the tide of the war turned, and victory was at hand, Dad apparently made a list of things he wanted to do when he got home. As he was processing out of the service, he wrote to Mom of his desire to settle down and have a family.

"I love you an awful lot," he wrote. "If you can ignore my ignorance, we'll get along just fine. I have a strong back and sturdy arms. I've been promised a job [in St. Paul, Minnesota] that pays $22.50 each and every week, sometimes with overtime pay, and soon it will pay all the way up to $30 per week.

By the way, I've even arranged for a house. I've already arranged to buy a nice 4 room house on Western Street for $17,532. The payments are only $87 per month … As I said before, I really love you. I'm from a good family, with no insanity, no syphilis, and everybody in my family lives a long life. Please meet me in Minnesota and give me a chance. If things work out—maybe, I hope, we can get married on October the 26th, 1946—if that's okay with you."

Signed, "Yours (if you want me), Jerome Smith, single, 28 yrs of age." With a P.S., "Enclosed is a picture of me so you will recognize me at the train depot."

My mom must have liked what she saw at the train depot that day. They got married, right on Dad's schedule, and started a family. Dad had no interest in going back to college. He must've felt that the war had already wasted enough of his time, and he wanted to get on with his life. He landed a job at the Post Office. As a letter carrier he got to wear a uniform, just like in the army; but nobody shot at him anymore. Some years later, he was awarded a supervisory position. After a month on this new job, however, he asked to get his old job back. He didn't like telling his friends what to do.

Mom had a baby every 18 months for the next 12 years. She might have had even more children except for the hysterectomy she needed—for "fibroids," she says. Eight hungry kids were quite a financial burden on a mailman's salary, so Mom went to work for the Post Office as well. The older girls took care of the younger kids while Mom was at work. Dad also did a variety of other jobs: janitor during the winter, groundskeeper in the summer, and landscaper during the spring and fall. Dad needed help with his part-time jobs, and that's where I (as first-born son) got involved with the family finances.

As a kid, I didn't know much about my parents. I knew my mom always wanted things to be better. I knew my dad always seemed tired. I also noticed that my dad's hands were rough from hard work, and his neck occasionally went into spasm. At the time I didn't know anything about his war injuries. I also didn't know his experience of seeing so many of his war buddies die had left Dad with a condition called "Shell Shock." A lifetime of counseling apparently didn't do much good. He had a small library of WW2 books, and spent many nights researching the war. He was never able to talk openly about these experiences, however.

Dad kept most of the promises he made to Mom. He was a good husband and father. He almost went crazy thinking about the war, though. He was a hard worker. He had many friends. He was admired for his honest and gentle nature. He never lied—except to hide how many extra loans he had taken out in order to make ends meet. And he wasn't able to keep his promise to live a long life.

In May of 1968, Dad was working especially hard. He was delivering mail in the day, and working on a big landscaping job in the evening. He had recently complained of chest pain. The doctor told Dad that "indigestion" was the cause of his chest pain. A heart test had been scheduled, but was cancelled. Dad resumed his landscaping work. The following morning he died of a heart attack.

At Dad's funeral, I said: "If I was the doctor, I would never let that happen." And that's when I decided I had to become a doctor. I'd never mess up like that. I promised that I would be better. I didn't want that to happen to anyone's dad.

3. Premorbid

"It's a big night tonight, boys" explained my first boss, Mr. Kildeer; "so do your best." He was instructing the kitchen crew at the *Hazelwood Bowl*. I was a busboy and dishwasher back then, but could feel excitement in the air as we prepared for a large dinner party. Mr. Kildeer had promised the Rotary Club that we could handle the dinner of one hundred people they anticipated. We were going to serve roast beef, mashed potatoes, coleslaw, rolls, relish trays, and chocolate cake. The cooks were in charge, of course; but we all needed to help in order to get the job done.

I was 14 years old. I didn't know much about restaurant work. To say I was naïve is an understatement. My friend, Bob Schultz, had helped me get the job. We both were dishwashers, but usually worked different nights. The Rotary Club banquet was a big deal, though; so we were both working that night. The head cook, Sam Dahl, gave us our job assignments. He told me to make the coleslaw. I was pleased that he gave me such an important job—but I had no idea how to do it. I asked the cook how to make coleslaw.

"You don't know how?" he said sarcastically. "How'd you get this job, anyway?" Maybe he didn't know I was only a dishwasher, I thought. I had my pride, so I told him I'd figure it out.

"Bob," I asked my friend, "Do you know how to make coleslaw?" He didn't know either. He had only been there a few weeks longer than me. We asked one of the waitresses. She gave us some ideas, and we winged it from there. We mixed cabbage, mayonnaise, vinegar, salt, and a little bit of mustard. It tasted pretty good to us. We mixed the ingredients together in a 5 gallon pail. It was hard to mix them with a spoon, so Bob just reached in there and mixed it with his bare hands.

"Did you wash your hands, Bill?" I asked.

"What's it to you, John? When I last washed my hands is none of your business."

"Oh, well … I just thought we should have clean hands before we touch food."

The head cook smiled as he overheard our conversation. He reminded us there was still a lot of work to do. We divided the coleslaw into serving bowls, two for each table. We also spooned up the potatoes, prepared the relish trays, and distributed baskets of rolls. We were proud to be cook's helpers. Then we distributed the platters of roast beef. Everything looked good and smelled great. Moments later the guests filed into the dining area, sat down, said a few words, and started eating.

We peeked into the room to see how things were going. Everything seemed to be going smoothly. Then we went back to the kitchen. Things were slow, but got busy again as the dinner was coming to an end. We had to get back to work, as well as get ready for the regular evening rush. Although we were good friends, Bob and I would race each other at bussing tables and washing dishes.

When the shift was coming to an end, the boss came into the kitchen. He congratulated everyone. And then he said:

"John, I heard you did an especially good job. I'm going to promote you to cook."

"Thanks, Mr. Kildeer," I said.

My friend, Bob, didn't look very happy. He glared at me. When we left work, he turned to me in anger, and said:

"John, you're such a brown nose. I can't believe you tried to show me up like that! And I'm the one who got you the job."

"You didn't get me the job. I got it myself. And maybe the boss noticed that I work harder than you … That's why *I* get to be a cook," I said.

Bob was jealous that I got promoted. We remained *friends*, but our *friendship* was never the same. I took advantage of my chance to be a cook. I learned as much as I could, and within a few weeks I was pretty good at turning out a variety of short order entrees. It wasn't long before Bob was also promoted to cook. He also learned fast, and became a decent cook. There was constant competition between us to see who could cook faster, flirt more with the waitresses, and get bigger tips.

School was like that, too. We were still friends, but we competed over everything. I got better grades than Bob. He resigned himself to the fact that I was the better student, so he tried to beat me in other areas. He was better than me in some sports; and I was better than him in others. And he was definitely the better partier. He was able to get alcohol from his older brother. That was a definite plus in attracting kids to his parties.

Bob and I parted company when I went off to college. I lost contact with other high school friends as well. Schoolwork became the most important thing in my life. I made friends with the people I lived with. I hadn't officially declared my major yet. I took a lot of premed classes, though; and secretly obsessed about becoming a doctor. A lot of premeds are that way. They don't divulge how desperately they want to become doctors. There are only so many slots for medical school admission, so nobody wanted to get their hopes up too high. Statistically, we knew that 2 out of 3 applicants to medical school would be rejected. It's no wonder that there's such fierce competition in premed classes. It's also not surprising that many *neurotic premeds* tend to keep to themselves.

My best premed friend was Jeff. He used to make fun of all the crazy premeds in the world. Premeds are students who are never happy with the way things are, go into the throes of depression if they don't get all *A's*, and try to act friendly despite their willingness to put a knife in your back—if it would improve their academic standing. I liked Jeff's unique sense of humor. I also felt comfortable around him—partly because I knew I was smarter than him; and knew he'd never get into medical school ahead of me. You see, *I was a crazy premed too*. My thinking was distorted just like every other crazy premed … Just like in my youth, I always wanted to do better than the other guy. I wanted to *look good* to people in authority.

Getting accepted to medical school was more of a relief than it was a joy. Rejection would have been a humility that was hard to bear. While I wanted to become a doctor, I didn't really know what that entailed. Most premeds don't have a clue what they're getting into.

Med school turned out to be four years of extremely hard work. A tremendous amount of information is force fed into medical students in a short period of time. It is assumed that if you are accepted into a reputable medical school, then you can handle the workload. Competition really doesn't need to be a part of in this environment, but *once a premed—always a premed.* Students start posturing for special honors, national board proficiency, and prestigious residencies. And so the competition to be the best continues long after it is really necessary.

Doctors are criticized for being hard to get along with. That shouldn't be surprising since premed training demands that you be competitive and self-serving. Medical school requires you to be a disciplined technocrat. Internships teach them how to take care of sick people. Student doctors certainly work hard for their degree, and deserve accolades for their accomplishments. Then medical residencies teach a body of knowledge specific to that specialty; and students learn a division of medical care into specialties that exaggerate their own importance, and denigrate other disciplines.

Compassion, cooperation and *communication* are not emphasized in medical school. *Competition* is emphasized to the extreme. Doctors have, by their nature, a *premorbid* tendency to be hard to get along with. They are rewarded for their ability to assimilate information. *Selfishness* is a useful—if not essential—characteristic of becoming a doctor.

Graduation Day June 14, 1980

"The Physician's Oath"

I swear by Apollo Physician, by Asclepius, by Health, by Panacea, and by all the gods and goddesses, making them my witnesses, that I will carry out, according to my ability and judgment, this oath and this indenture ... I will use treatment to help the sick ... never with a view to injury ... I will keep pure and holy both my life and my art ... In whatsoever houses I enter, I will enter to help the sick, and I will abstain from all intentional wrongdoing and harm, especially from abusing the bodies of man or woman, bond or free. And whatsoever I shall see or hear in the course of my profession in my intercourse with men, if it be what should not be published abroad, I will never divulge, holding such things to be holy secrets. Now if I carry out this oath, and break it not, may I gain forever reputation among all men for my life and my art; but if I transgress it and forswear myself, may the opposite befall me.

Hippocrates, "The Physician's Oath,"
translated by WHS Jones, Loeb Classical Library.

4. Bad Doctor

The young doctor entered the hospital with bravado. He was a doctor-in-training who was moonlighting for the weekend. His job was to cover the emergency room of Barnsville, a small town in Montana, in order to give old Dr. Bridgestone a few days off. As a student at the University, he felt his training had prepared him to handle any problem that might come through the doors of this hick hospital.

"I'm Dr. Sillicon," he said to the patient. "What can I do for you?"

"It's my cough, Doc. It's just not getting any better," said the young woman. "I saw Dr. Bridgestone last week, but the antibiotic he gave me hasn't helped." She was obviously anxious about the problem. Her name was Jennifer. She appeared in good general health. She was 34 years old, didn't smoke, and had never really been sick before. Dr. Bridgestone had told her she had pneumonia, but hadn't ordered an X-ray to confirm the diagnosis.

"He didn't get an X-ray?" Dr. Sillicon asked with derision. "How can he say it was pneumonia without an X-ray?" Dr Sillicon's comment made the woman even more anxious. She started to doubt her regular doctor's competence. Although Dr. Bridgestone had taken care of her since she was a baby, he did appear more tired lately; and perhaps his medical skills were eroding with the passage of time. Dr. Bridgestone had to see over 30 patients a day in his clinic, and often skipped X-rays when he knew what was going on. He also knew that Jennifer's cough would take more than a few days to get better. He considered giving her asthma meds, but wanted to see how she did on antibiotics alone. Dr. Bridgestone told her to come back next week. She wasn't happy with how things were going, though. That's why she went to the ER that weekend. She wanted another doctor's opinion on why she was still sick.

Dr. Sillicon ordered an X-ray. When it came back (about an hour later) he noticed a clouded area on the film. He told her that the X-ray was consistent with pneumonia. It also could represent a congenital anomaly, sarcoidosis, pneumo-coniosis, or possibly even neoplasm.

"I don't know what any of those words mean," Jennifer said. "The only word I've even heard of is 'neoplasm'—what is that?"

"Neoplasm is 'lung cancer,'" Sillicon replied. "Although it's not likely, it needs to be kept in the differential diagnosis."

Jennifer's anxiety level went through the roof. The only thing she remembers from that day is that the smart young doctor said she might have "lung cancer." Her cough got even worse. She immediately blamed Dr. Bridgestone for wasting valuable time in delaying her cancer diagnosis and treatment.

Dr. Sillicon told her she needed a battery of tests. In the next few months, Jennifer had four more chest X-rays, two CAT scans, a lung scan, pulmonary function tests, and numerous blood tests. Since she no longer trusted Dr. Bridgestone, she went to a neighboring city for her evaluation. The doctor there agreed with Dr. Bridgestone's initial diagnosis of pneumonia, but he didn't want to be sued—so he ordered multiple tests to *rule out* something more serious. Asthma meds were started. She continued her antibiotics. Her cough and anxiety gradually improved. She couldn't sleep at night. She could still hear Dr. Sillicon's words in her head: "You might have lung cancer."

Dr. Sillicon, for his part, felt like he did his job. He never wanted to miss anything. He felt it was his obligation to tell patients all the diagnostic possibilities. In order to be complete, he didn't mind disagreeing with *local doctors* who didn't know as much as he did. He felt there was a great opportunity to update the medical care in a small town like Barnsville, so decided to move there. He knew he could make a lot of money there. There wouldn't be any real competition for his expert services.

Dr. Bridgestone warmly welcomed Dr. Sillicon to Barnsville. He was glad to have the help. Dr. Bridgestone didn't even mind that many of his patients switched their care to Dr. Sillicon. That was their prerogative, he figured; and he was too tired to worry about it. It took a while for Dr. Bridgestone to realize that Dr. Sillicon was criticizing his care. He wasn't too happy about that.

It took Jennifer a year to get over her fear that she might have lung cancer. She never went back to Dr. Bridgestone. She was fortunate to find a doctor in the neighboring city who was eventually able to reassure her that there wasn't anything seriously wrong with her. She continued to have asthma, however. Every time she caught a cold she had a lingering cough that required inhalers (and other meds) to get better.

[Senior devil instructing his student:]

"How much better for us if *all* humans died in costly nursing homes amid doctors who lie, nurses who lie, friends who lie, as we have trained them, promising life to the dying, encouraging the belief that sickness excuses every indulgence, and even, if our workers know their job, withholding all suggestion of a priest lest it should betray to the sick man his true condition!"

C.S. Lewis, The Screwtape Letters, C. 1963, Macmillan Publishing Company, pp 26-27.

5. Good Doctor

The sound of the birds chirping awoke me that morning. A cool autumn breeze blew in from the open motel window. A wispy layer of morning fog hovered over a nearby field. As I drank my morning coffee, the sights and sounds of morning traffic revealed the vibrant small town of Twin Junction, Montana. My wife and I were visiting, and wondered if we could live in this town. We had narrowed our choice between Twin Junction and Barnsville, a neighboring town. This was our second trip to the area. My mind was full of anticipation. I knew it was an important day in our lives. I suspected it would be a day we would long remember.

My wife and I dressed in silence, and then we went to get something to eat. We wanted to start the day out right. The motel clerk recommended that we go to the "Double D" Restaurant, which was a favorite place for people to eat, drink coffee, and just hang out. The second generation of the Donaldson family was running the place. The smell of freshly baked caramel rolls helped us find the door, and seemed to beckon us to join the morning crowd who gathered there. They served breakfast all day long. Their lunch and dinner specials were also reputed to be tasty and affordable. My wife loved her Belgian waffle with strawberries. I had a ham and cheese omelet, and it was as tasty as any I'd ever had.

We pictured ourselves living in Twin Junction. I was to be the new doctor in town. I was recruited because the two primary care doctors there were overwhelmed with their patient load, and genuinely hoped we would move to town. The hospital also hoped that I would modernize their Intensive Care Unit.

As we were finishing our breakfast, the hospital administrator, Ricky Weeks, entered the restaurant. Spying us at our table, he greeted us loudly:

"Doctor Smith, Mrs. Smith, how nice it is to see you." We stood to greet him. He vigorously shook our hands. "How was your trip? We're so glad a doctor of your immense quality has decided to move to our great little town."

The people at the restaurant were all looking at us. We quietly said our trip was okay. As we all sat down, my wife and I noticed that people were still looking at us. Their stares were not unfriendly, but we weren't used to all the attention. We had been to Twin Junction once before, but that trip was incognito. This was a *second look* trip. I had been impressed by the hospital facility, and thought it would be a good place to practice medicine. My wife wasn't sure that she wanted to leave the comfort of her life in Fargo, North Dakota, however.

My wife, Grace, didn't think much of the houses we had looked at during our last visit. She shuddered to think that we would have to move from our Victorian-style home in Fargo to a mundane house in the middle of nowhere. Mr. Weeks had arranged for us to meet a different realtor this time. Her name was Marlene Beagle, and she was waiting by the restaurant cashier. She warmly greeted us as we approached the register.

As I attempted to pay the $15 breakfast bill, Mr. Weeks insisted on picking up the tab.

"Charge it to the hospital," he told the cashier. "I don't want the Smiths to think we're cheap."

Marlene Beagle knew of a house that my wife might like. It was known as "the old Kasselback House." It was an older home with a storied past. Many famous people had lived and died there. Grace loved the place! She was impressed by its stately appearance. As we were walking up the front walk, Grace's enthusiasm for the house couldn't be contained. She told the realtor we just had to buy the place. The sale was made before we even entered the house.

The decision as to where we would live was made at that precise moment. My intention had been to weigh the pros and cons of offers that would be made to me, but that was no longer necessary. My wife decided that we should live in this grand old house. That's all there was to it.

The inside of the house was nice. I especially admired the fireplace. The previous owners had ripped out the kitchen cupboards and bathroom fixtures, however. I knew there would be disadvantages to buying an older home. This one was truly charming, however. It had nice woodwork, imported tin ceilings, and was located next to a park. I just chuckle when I think how the decision was made to move to Twin Junction. My wife decided that we must turn this old house into our home.

My wife and I came back to town a few months later. This time it was for keeps. We had a moving van full of all our belongings. I was scheduled to open my office on the following

Monday, January 6, 1986. It was the weekend. We were unloading boxes when a policeman came to the door ...

"Are you the new doctor?" he asked.

"Yes, I'm Dr. Smith," I said. "What's the problem?"

"They need you at the hospital—right now!"

I left the unpacking duties to my wife, and followed the police car to the hospital. It was the first of hundreds of high speed trips I was to make on that road. When I got there, I was directed to the Intensive Care Unit (ICU), where a team of health care workers were gathered around a thirty year-old woman who was on the verge of dying.

"Are you Dr Smith?" asked Nurse White.

"Yes, what's going on?"

"We need your help on this patient." Nurse White gave me a quick summary. The patient had taken some pills that had been prescribed by a doctor from another town. She was apparently trying to kill herself. The patient had been awake and stable when she was brought to the hospital. Then she got sleepy; and soon thereafter she went into a full coma. Her vital signs crashed: the nurses were not able to get a pulse or blood pressure reading. Her family doctor was Doctor Goodyear. He had been in and out of the ICU, ordered several interventions, but nothing worked. Nurse White could tell Dr. Goodyear was in over his head. She got permission to bring in "the new doctor" on the case.

"Why aren't you doing CPR?" I asked.

"Because she has a normal tracing on the cardiac monitor," another nurse said. It was Nurse Black, and she apparently carried some weight in local nurse politics.

"That's not good enough. Start CPR!" I said. "She's in *EMD*," I added, meaning *Electromechanical Dissociation*. EMD is a condition where the patient has a rhythm on the cardiac monitor but doesn't have adequate mechanical heart function. It's now called *Pulseless Electrical Activity*. Whatever you call it, it needs to be treated as a full code.

I placed a tube down her windpipe to help her breathe. She still had a good tracing on the cardiac monitor. We still could not get a pulse or blood pressure, however. Chest compressions were started. IV fluids were ordered. I tried to gather a quick summary of why she was in this *near-death* situation.

"Does she have any known medical problems?" I asked.

"She's been depressed. She had a baby six months ago," Nurse White said.

I was trying to put the pieces of a puzzle together. It's the way doctors must take care of extremely sick patients. Emergency treatment must start before the doctor knows exactly what's going on. Sometimes you have to take your best guess, and then follow your instincts.

"Give her four amps of sodium bicarbonate," I ordered.

"You've got to be kidding! We're not supposed to use Bicarb anymore," Nurse Black said in a condescending manner.

"Who says so?" I asked.

"The latest *ACLS* algorithms," she responded. She was, of course, referring to the *Advanced Cardiac Life Support* guidelines, which are revised every few years.

"I know the guidelines. I've been a certified ACLS instructor since 1981. This patient isn't on the algorithm, though. Bicarb may be her only chance. With her postpartum depression, I suspect she has taken a lethal tricyclic antidepressant overdose. Bicarb is how we save these patients," I explained.

The woman's family doctor was back in the room. He appeared fidgety and uncomfortable with the situation.

"*Doctor* Smith wants to give her *Bicarb*," Nurse Black said sarcastically. "Is that okay with you?"

He looked at me. I shook my head affirmatively. He looked back at the nurses. "I guess so," he replied.

The Bicarb was given. Within minutes her pulse and blood pressure were restored. It was like magic. The patient didn't wake up, however.

"She's probably *brain dead* by now," Nurse Black said. She was still being frosty with me. She apparently didn't want to acknowledge that a rookie doctor knew something that she didn't. What she didn't know was that I had been a doctor for six years, and had a total of 14 years of *doctor training* under my belt. I had paid my dues. My education had prepared me well for the medical challenges of small town medicine.

"We'll see," I replied. I didn't know how long the patient had ineffective breathing and blood pressure. I know that just a few minutes of cardiac arrest can result in brain death, but this was not the time to give up on her. This young woman was a wife and mother. Hopefully she had more reserve than most cardiac arrest victims. We had to "hope for the best but prepare for the worst," which is also what I told the family.

It took a few days for the patient to wake up. Her left side didn't move normally. The lack of oxygen had taken its toll, but the patient and her family were grateful she had improved. They were glad that she was alive. The woman smiled at her family, and cried when she realized how close she had come to dying.

The woman's left-sided weakness resolved over the next few months. Her depression still needed treatment, however. I gave her only limited quantities of her antidepressant medicine—so she couldn't hurt herself. She had another episode of postpartum depression after her next baby was born. It was treated in a safe and effective manner. She had *recurring postpartum depression*, which is due to a known biochemical imbalance ... She wasn't a bad person. Her depression was not because she had character weakness, lack of intelligence, or disturbed childhood. She had a disease that needed treatment—just like any other illness.

I felt great satisfaction to have been able to help this woman. I was fortunate to have been in the *right place* at the *right time* with the *right knowledge*. God gave me that opportunity and responsibility. That's the greatest joy that a physician can experience.

The hospital learned that I knew a thing or two about medicine. Doctor Goodyear and Nurse White thanked me for helping out on the case. Nurse Black didn't say anything, though. She scowled at me every time we passed in the hallway. I suppose she thinks I was trying to show her up. That's not the case. I was, in fact, just trying to help the patient.

Life Can Be Messy ...

6. Growing Pains

In the next few years, my practice grew by leaps and bounds. Word got out that I knew how to take care of complicated medical problems. It's true: I did feel comfortable in the ICU, and I saved patients that many doctors would not have known how to manage. I was well-trained, and that provided me with cognitive knowledge and procedural skills that were lacking in most small towns. In other words, it was expected that I know how to take care of these patients. It was my job; and if I couldn't figure out what was going on, then I was morally and professionally obligated to send these patients to someone who could.

I enjoyed the challenge of taking care of ICU patients—heart attacks, heart failure, breathing problems, severe infections, and the like. Taking care of these patients took a lot of time and energy, though. It meant being on call 24 hours a day. It meant getting phone calls in the middle of the night to answer nurse questions. It meant dealing with a multitude of problems that intensive care patients have. As a young doctor, I enjoyed the challenge. As time went by, it became more of a burden. It became harder to have both a professional and a personal life. It became hard to please everyone: the patient, their family, hospital staff, and my own family.

A few years after we moved to Twin Junction, we were blessed with the birth of a son. Within a few more years, sons number two and number three were born. This sudden fertility came as a bit of a surprise. Just a few years earlier, a big city doctor had told my wife she might not be able to have any children, and we should think about adoption.

With our new family life, my wife said I needed to work less. At the age of 30, I didn't think it was any big deal to work 80 hours a week. By the age 35, I tried to slow down to 60 hours a week. At the age of 40 my own doctor told me to work no more than 40 hours per week. He warned me I could lose everything if I didn't. I didn't believe him. I also knew it was impossible to do that in a small town, a place where weekend call alone is 60 hours long.

I didn't spend enough time *having fun*. For example, I paid for a membership at the Country Club year after year—but golfed only a few times a year. Despite the fact that I rarely golfed, I would get frustrated if my scores weren't improving. In a similar way, I bought a shotgun (at a friend's insistence) but rarely went hunting. And when I coached my kids' sports teams (baseball, soccer, basketball, and flag football) I was accused of being too *competitive* … Kids' sports are not supposed to fixate on winning.

I enjoyed running. At least I think I did. Over my lifetime, I've spent a lot of time running. I told myself that running is both the *cause of* and the *cure for* exhaustion. It was an amazing phenomenon. I'd come home from work, put on my running clothes, and be out the door within minutes. I didn't have to go to the gym or wait around for anyone in order to get my endorphin fix. And I had the uncanny ability to run a quick five miles without any training. Once a year I'd increase my mileage to 8-10 mile runs, a few times a week, and then complete 26.2 mile marathons in Minnesota. I ran eleven of these marathons. The friend that I did marathons with would run 60 miles per week to train. Even though he trained ten times harder than me, during the race we had about the same endurance.

Running marathons is essentially a reflection of my life. I usually run alone. I train alone. In marathons the runner is surrounded by thousands of other runners, but essentially runs alone. And that's how it was to practice medicine in a small town. Patients flocked into my office to get much-needed medical services. I was expected to move from one patient to the next every fifteen minutes. If I slowed down, I'd throw the schedule off for the day. The other doctors in town were equally busy. We were all solo practitioners. We interacted (when necessary) on medical matters, but didn't socialize much. We didn't need to compete with each other—but did. We were still acting like *premeds*. We hurried through our daily routine, running from dawn to dusk to meet the challenges of the day.

My practice was a financial success. For several years I was in the top 1% of gross revenue for similar practices (Internal Medicine) around the country. This specialty is one of the lowest paid specialties in medicine, however. I was making ten times more than my father ever made. My wife and I felt wealthy—even though we had a pile of debt. We went to medical conferences around the country, stayed in fancy hotels, and ate at the finest restaurants. My wife was able to buy a lot of clothes. We were able to buy nice things for our home. And with the recent arrival of our children, we felt we were on the top of the world.

7. Turning Point

I was in the habit of eating breakfast at the "Double D" restaurant on at least a weekly basis. It was just another Monday morning when I sat down at my usual table, placed an order for a ham and cheese omelet, and enjoyed a few cups of coffee. Within just a few minutes, I said "Hi" to about a dozen or so familiar faces. Many of them were my patients.

"Eggs again, Doc?" asked the banker. "I thought we're not supposed to eat food like that."

"Everything in moderation," I replied. I tried not to look up. I didn't want to spoil the taste of my high fat breakfast.

"Practice what you preach," he said.

"I never said …" But the point was lost. He was out the door.

In walked Dick Williams, one of the local dentists. We were friends. He sat down at my table, ordered coffee and a roll, and said:

"Make it quick," he told the waitress. "I have to get to work."

"Dick, how have you been?" I asked.

"Busy, busy, busy … Money, money, money. Cavities are good for business. Whoever said sweets are bad—was wrong," he chuckled.

"Don't rub it in," I replied. "I know you make more money than me. But think of the glamour of my position compared to yours …"

"Yeah," he snickered. "Being a GP in this town is really glamorous. You get to take care of sore throats, back pain, and high blood pressure all day. At least I get to fill cavities and apply teeth whiteners."

"Mundane as it sounds, it is a living," I replied. "Disease and dental decay pay the bills. Besides that, I'm not just a GP. At least I have job security, right?"

"Yeah, right," he responded. "You shouldn't get over-confident," he added. "Did you hear what happened to Doc Jones in Barnsville?"

"No. What happened?"

"Some woman charged him with 'inappropriate touching.' He has to defend himself before the Board. He's lost a lot of patients over the rumor of what he might have done. I heard he's leaving the state."

"Did he do it?" I asked.

"It doesn't matter if he did anything or not," the dentist said. "His career is over."

Our conversation came to a glum conclusion. We knew that as public figures, especially as health care providers, our reputation was everything. If something like that could happen in Barnsville, then it could happen in Twin Junction. We didn't have as much job security as we thought.

With that sobering thought, I finished my breakfast, and then hurried to my office. In spite of what people say about doctors, we really don't like being late. It just happens. When

Mrs. Olson brought in her son Jimmy for his earache that morning, for instance, I wound up seeing—and treating—the entire family. Five for the price of one. It's hard for patients to pass up those deals.

I was late for my next appointment. I was, in fact, late for everything that day. Most people tolerate a doctor's tendency to be a little late. Some even understand that we have little or no control over our daily schedule. And days when I had to cover the emergency room (ER) were even worse. That day was particularly memorable. I was on call for the ER, and had three patients in the office and four in the ER at the same time. Kendra Black, the bossy ER nurse, had zero appreciation for the situation, and expected me to see everybody at the same time.

Mr. Peterson, a middle-aged farmer, came to the office for evaluation of occasional "indigestion." The suspicious thing about his discomfort was that it only occurred when he lifted things. He would perspire and feel dizzy with these episodes. Although he hadn't had any of this discomfort for the last few days, I could tell it bothered him. His wife was there with him. The last doctor he saw gave him something for his stomach, but it didn't help. I ordered an EKG and some blood tests. I suspected he was having *Angina pectoris*, and knew he needed more treatment.

I was called *stat* to the ER. The patient there was having a massive heart attack. He could barely speak. He had severe chest pain, was sweating profusely, had labored breathing, and his blood pressure was low. There was a reasonably good response to my initial treatment. There was still a chance that he might need to be put on a breathing machine. Immediate stabilization and transfer to the ICU was needed.

Meanwhile, back in the office, Mr. Peterson's tests showed that he previously had a small heart attack. He didn't know when. It might have been when he had "the flu" a few months ago, when he was fixing farm equipment. I gave him aspirin and Lopressor in the office. I made a phone call to the cardiologist, and arranged for him to get a heart catherization.

Meanwhile, back in the ER, a kid walked in with a sore ankle. He had twisted it yesterday while playing kickball. His mother noticed it was swollen, and wanted it immediately evaluated.

Fred Gladiolus was also in the ER. Fred had more money than he knew what to do with. Previously a hard worker, he had oil discovered on his farm. He no longer had to work. He filled his idle time by drinking Brandy Manhattan's. His blood pressure was difficult to control; and it got worse according to how much drinking he did. Recently he also developed "Holiday Heart Syndrome." His heart would race after binges of drinking. He resented my advice that he should cut down on alcohol. He said it was my fault that he felt bad, and that he had to take too many medications. Today his heart was racing and needed immediate treatment. He was groggy and smelled of alcohol—even though it was 10 a.m. I ordered medication. His heart rate improved. When Fred woke up enough to recognize me, he glared at me, and said:

"Get out of here, you SOB. You're the one who caused my heart condition. You've been poisoning me with your God damn drugs. I wouldn't let you take care of my dog!"

I guess that meant I was fired. Another doctor was called to continue his care. Swallowing my pride, I left the room without comment.

Meanwhile, back in the office, two patients, who had been waiting for an hour, agreed to come back next week. They understood. Chris, my office nurse, took care of their immediate needs. My office staff, realizing that I would be tied up in the hospital, cancelled the rest of the morning's appointments. My own patients, the ones I had known and treated for years, had no trouble adjusting to the inconvenience. The situation was handled diplomatically.

Meanwhile, back in the ER, the kid with the sprained ankle was still waiting. I quickly evaluated him. I agreed with him that it was, indeed, a sprained ankle. He seemed fine with the situation. His mother, however, was upset that they had been waiting for over an hour. She wanted an X-ray. I told her I didn't think it was necessary.

"As you can see, things are pretty hectic around here," I tried to explain.

"I don't care," she replied. "We came here for an X-ray."

"I'll have the nurse give him an ankle wrap and crutches. Even though he walked in on it, he should try to stay off that ankle for a few days. You can see your regular doctor if he's not getting better," I said. With that, I left the exam area. I had to get back to my sick patients. Some people are not going to be made happy, I realized.

Nurse Black went to talk to the mother. She told the mother that I hadn't spent much time with them. She put on the ankle wrap and dispensed crutches. She did her job, I guess, but also encouraged the mother to file a formal complaint against me.

"That doctor is always in a hurry. I think he's rude. I don't like him," said Nurse Black. "If you file an official complaint, the hospital administrator will have to discipline him." She helped the woman fill out the complaint. A clinic doctor was able to see the boy later that day. The mother got the X-ray she wanted, and it was negative. The doctor agreed with me: it was a minor ankle sprain, and an ankle wrap and rest were all that was needed.

Some days working in the ER can be downright dangerous: threats against a doctor's life occasionally occur. One time a psychotic patient stole a gun, and told people he was going to kill his brother-in-law. I was asked to provide medical intervention. The man then decided that he also had to kill me. On another occasion, a body builder (and suspected steroid user) was mad that I told him to find another doctor. He called me "an arrogant prick" and promised he would "get me." Three witnesses told the hospital administrator of his threats against me. In the first case, antipsychotic medications provided immense benefit for the man; and we subsequently became friends. The other man's words were ignored; and he has continued to make threats against me.

It's good to have brothers ...

8. Endless Vacation

It was a cool August morning. The fog rolled across the still waters of Eagle Lake. The silence of the morning was broken by the crows cawing at each other. The sweet music of songbirds could also be heard, if you listened, and sharply contrasted the belligerent cacophony of the crows.

John was the first one up that day, and he heard the call of the birds. He sat on the deck chair, scanned the lake, and pondered the world. How different this was from most of his mornings, he thought. He mused that the things we see every day are often not noticed. The pace of this week's vacation was certainly different from his usual routine; and he was trying to appreciate things he usually ignored.

The fog was moving in on him now. His view became clouded. It made him a little bit nervous. It was surprisingly cold for a summer morning. The gray sky blended in with the gray lake. There was no horizon to discriminate the sky from the earth.

Doctor John was on a much-needed vacation, but he knew it was coming to an end. Next week he would be back to his usual routine: phone calls all day and night, running from the office to the hospital, trying to keep everyone happy. He treated a variety of conditions—mostly simple but some serious problems. John's job, he realized, was to cure the sick and afflict the cured (with health advice). That was sometimes harder than people thought. He had been at this for 25 years now, and the job was starting to wear him down.

This was the first summer vacation he had taken in years. This week also felt like work: he was supposed to make his wife and kids happy. His wife, Grace, had a list of all the things she wanted to do. She was good at planning their social calendar, she often said; and besides, John didn't know how to work out these details.

Grace said they should visit her mother. They did. Grace said they should visit her high school friend. They did. John wanted to see an old college friend, but it was (she said) too far out of the way. They visited Grace's step-brother instead.

Grace's step-brother, Matt Brown, was a nice enough guy. He had this lake cabin. Actually, it was his wife's father's cabin; but it was nice anyway.

John, Grace and their three sons arrived at the cabin a few days ago. Matt and his wife, Jane, greeted them as they pulled up the driveway. The boys got along fairly well with Susan, Jane's daughter from her second marriage. Grace and Matt got along famously. They hugged and chatted without end. John and Jane, who didn't know each other, politely stood by and attempted small talk.

John felt like it was always this way when Grace visited her friends and family. He tried to make the best of it.

"Nice place you got here," John said to Jane.

"Thank you. It's actually my father's place, but he lets us use it, providing we don't break anything," she replied.

"How long has your family had this place?" John asked.

"Almost thirty years now," she replied. "Daddy bought it after he made his first million."

"What line of work is your father in?" John asked.

"Real estate," Jane said.

Matt, Jane's husband, was a part-time carpenter. Jane worked for her father. On their own, they never could afford such a luxurious vacation home. Jane's father was always generous; but he secretly thought his daughter could have done better. Despite this drawback, Matt was much-loved by family and friends alike.

Grace noticed John chatting, and asked:

"What are you two talking about?"

"Nothing much," John said.

"No, really—what are you talking about? Is it a secret?" Grace asked.

"The weather," Jane replied.

"Of course," Grace responded. "John always talks about the weather."

"Speaking of the weather," Matt added, "we should take the boat out. It's getting late in the season, and you never know when the weather will turn bad."

And that's just what they did. They boated from one end of the lake to the other, pulled the kids on the tube, and had a great time. It was a gorgeous lake and a perfect day. The lakeshore was dotted with expensive homes. Matt, Jane, and Susan seemed accustomed to the luxury of the lake life. John's family, on the other hand, lived more modestly. The boys had a wonderful time. Grace seemed to be enjoying herself, but occasionally looked to John as if there was something on her mind.

Dinner was very nice. Jane and Matt treated them to a meal of steak, fish, wild rice, and corn on the cob. The adults drank wine; and the kids drank fruit punch. Despite a comment from Grace to "watch his cholesterol," John enjoyed the feast tremendously.

After dinner, when they were alone, Grace approached John in a serious manner, asking:

"John, why can't we have a place like this? As a doctor, you should be able to afford something nice …"

"I'm just a country doctor," he replied. "You know I don't make that much money. We're not done paying off all our loans."

"You can't take it with you," Grace said. "You know, John, today could be the last day of your life. The kids and I would love a place like this. Besides that, you need to relax more. Living by the lake might be good for your blood pressure."

"You're right, Grace. You're always right. A place like this would be wonderful. And I know I won't live forever. At least I've got good life insurance. So if I die you and the kids will be able to live in style," he said sarcastically.

John didn't say anything more. Grace didn't say anything either. They gave each other the silent treatment, and went to bed—one mad at the other, and *vice versa*. John couldn't sleep that night. He felt like a failure. He couldn't provide his wife and kids with the lifestyle they longed for.

It was now the morning after. John leaned back in the deck chair. The gray sky and fog temporarily clouded his thinking.

Should he be mad at Grace for asking for something they couldn't afford? Maybe she didn't know. Maybe she and the kids just didn't understand the family finances. Why weren't they ever content? Were they spoiled? He never had such luxuries as a child, he recalled; and that never hurt him.

The vacation was coming to an end. John felt bad that he had to pack up the family and head back home. He had to get back to work. Summer vacation was not over for his family, though. It seemed like they were always on vacation, he thought.

Doctor John returned to work the following Monday. Missing a week at the office meant a double workload upon his return. He rushed from patient to patient. He dealt with their ailments as well as he could. Several patients were mad that he was gone last week, when they needed him the most.

John didn't have time for a lunch break. He sucked down a Coke and gobbled a donut as he read the office mail—which was mostly bills. He realized he didn't have the good health habits that he recommends to his patients.

The afternoon schedule was also overbooked. Rushing from patient to patient, he started having indigestion. He blamed his diet. Antacids didn't seem to help, though.

"I need a vacation," John said to himself. But then he remembered that he had just returned from one.

John wondered why the discomfort in his chest wasn't going away. He hoped it was indigestion, but started to wonder if it was something else. And so he went into one of the exam rooms, locked the door, took off his shirt, and did an EKG on himself. He was sweating profusely by now. His chest pain was worse. The EKG showed, as he suspected, that he was having a heart attack.

John wondered if it was too late for him to get healthy. He needed help—but remembered that he had locked the door. He was feeling weaker now. His pulse was irregular, and then the heart monitor showed Ventricular Tachycardia.

"I should've taken another vacation," John said out loud. He was delirious now. He felt the pain in his chest in a detached manner. His breathing was labored. His pulse was weak. He knew he was going to die.

"I guess I'm gonna' get that vacation after all," he said. The monitor showed he was going into Ventricular Fibrillation. "It might be—an endless vacation...."

Is it the end? Or a new beginning?

9. Starting Over

Chris, the office nurse, knocked on the door. It was still locked. Then she pounded on the door, and yelled:

"Are you okay? Doc! Are you in there? What's going on?"

There was no answer. She knew there was something wrong. She found the master key, and opened the exam room door. She found Doctor Smith's lifeless body on the exam table. He wasn't responding. He had no pulse. He wasn't breathing. She screamed: "Code Blue! Call the Code Team! Bring me the Crash Cart!"

Her moves were quick. She was nervous, but she knew what to do. She placed the electrode patches on his chest, and ran 300 joules of electricity through him. His body jumped. His cardiac monitor had shown Ventricular Fibrillation, but now returned to Normal Sinus Rhythm. John woke up. His breathing and pulse normalized. Just like that, a life had been saved. Prompt treatment of *Cardiac Arrest* can make all the difference in the world.

Doctor John Smith was now Patient Smith. He was no longer in control. A team of workers gave him oxygen, started an intravenous line, undressed him, and moved him to the hospital. His heart rhythm was monitored. It only took one shock to bring him back to life, but there was danger that he could slip away again—if everything wasn't done correctly.

He was brought to the ICU. A blood clot had blocked one of his coronary arteries. A blood thinner was given to dissolve the clot. The medicine worked. His EKG showed dramatic improvement. Other treatment was also given.

John hated being a patient. Considering the alternative (of being six feet under) he should have been more grateful. The reality of his condition hadn't completely sunk in. He was dead, and now was alive. That's the way it was, his doctor told him. And then he started to appreciate the true nature of the problem. In the following few days he personally thanked everyone in the hospital for their help. He thanked the nurses, doctor, ward clerk, X-ray technician, lab technician, engineers, janitors, and cooks. He was especially grateful to Chris, his office nurse, who had the courage to break into the locked room, call for help, and defibrillate his dying heart.

Later John went to a big city where he underwent a heart catheterization. The study showed relatively mild Coronary Artery Disease. Surgery wasn't needed. He had to take several medications, though. He needed to control his risk factors. He needed to reduce his stress level.

A *near death* experience can change your outlook toward life. Doctor John had seen it happen to hundreds of his patients, and now he knew what it was like. Some things became more important—like his relationship with God and family matters. Other things became less important. John tried to sort out his priorities in life.

John knew there were people he had offended. Even if previous disagreements had been two-sided, he now made apologies for "his part" to as many people as he could. If he

were to die tomorrow, he didn't want to go to his grave knowing he should have made amends to someone who felt hurt by
his words or deeds. Some people took this as an admission
that John had been *wrong* in everything he had ever done.
That's not how John saw it. He was just acknowledging that
he didn't always do or say the right thing. He didn't always
know a person's special needs. Sometimes he didn't even
know they were offended. Sometimes he didn't care. He came
to realize that he couldn't please everyone—he never could in
the past, and never would be able to in the future.

Because of his heart attack, John didn't work for a few
weeks. When he returned to his job, his workload was
restricted. People thought he was a changed man. John was
relaxed and pleasant to be around. He loved everyone. He was
fun. As time went on, work demands increased to previous (if
not greater) levels. His temperament gradually soured. His
wife was the first to notice:

"John," his wife inquired: "Are you on drugs? Some days
you are so pleasant. Other times you're just like before—irritable and demanding. What's going on?"

"I *am not* on drugs. I resent the implication. Maybe I
should be, though. Everyone expects me to be perfect.
Everyone wants a piece of me. I'm tired, Grace," he said. It
looked as if he might cry. He looked Grace in the eye, and
added: "Nobody can keep up the pace of life that I've had. It's
just a matter of time before I go *completely crazy*—or have
another heart attack."

Grace tried to understand. Years of arguing with John had
clouded her perspective. His recent heart attack had changed

all that. She still loved him. They were, after all, still married. And now his admission of imperfection made him more likeable. He was, she realized, just a human being—complete with strengths and weaknesses. His vulnerability was appealing. It made her want to help him.

10. Crazy Like Me

John surprised his wife by agreeing to see a psychiatrist. Grace said they needed help. They argued about everything. John hoped the shrink would say his wife was the one with a problem. But he had already sent her to three different therapists, and it hadn't made him any better. His knew his irritability was getting worse; it was causing difficulties both at work and at home.

Doctor John was always in a hurry. He slowed down after his heart attack, but within a few months he was back to his old self. If he didn't try his hardest, then something might go wrong. And John enjoyed the accolades he got for the work he did. Work results were, he figured, how people should be judged. "Never mind how you do it—just do it." That's what he has been told. And people expect good results from their doctor.

John worked hard. He worried a lot. He had trouble sleeping at night. He thought all night about what happened that day, and wondered what might happen the next day. He used alcohol to help him sleep. He never drank before midnight; and he only drank (he told himself) because he needed it—to help him sleep and worry less.

"Alcohol has never made me sick," John would brag, so he didn't think he could be an alcoholic. Alcohol used to make him feel good. In recent years, it only lessened his malaise. In truth, alcohol was poison to his system; it made him restless, irritable, and discontent.

John's mother-in-law, Brenda, *just knew* he was an alcoholic. She tried to educate Grace on the matter. Brenda and Grace had been discussing John's mental health for many years:

"If he would just admit that he was an alcoholic," Brenda used to say; "then he would have a chance to get better. I know about alcoholism. My dad and brother were alcoholics."

"Maybe it's just a *drinking problem*," Grace used to say. "Sometimes he controls his drinking without difficulty."

"That doesn't mean anything," Brenda would reply. "I can see you need to learn about alcoholism. Here—let me find you some books on the subject."

Without hesitation, Brenda pulled out a stack of paperback books on how to sober up an alcoholic, how to live with an alcoholic, and a variety of other "How To" books. She was a veritable expert on the subject. Her home library of paperback books had made her so.

But that was years ago. John hasn't had a drink since 1992. He surprised his wife and mother-in-law by going to alcoholism treatment, and by staying sober. John and his mother-in-law get along better than they used to, but he doesn't appreciate her tendency to use pop psychology and religion to explain every problem in the world.

John always wanted to do his best. When he was good, he wanted to be better. But when things didn't go well, in one way or another, he felt terrible. And he hated it when people around him messed up. Even if the results were good, he hated to be criticized for some detail of the process. And being sensitive to criticism was difficult in John's profession. As a medical doctor for 25 years, John couldn't help but have a few people dislike him. People could take offense if he told them to lose weight or stop smoking. Giving a nurse a "Doctor's Order" wasn't always given (or received) with diplomacy. But his eccentricities were labeled *bad* without any qualifications. In small towns doctors can't help but attract attention. This can be like living under a microscope. And if you get on someone's bad side—in a small town or elsewhere—there is inevitable gossip as to "what a jerk" that guy is.

Doctor John wanted people to like him. He spent way too much time worrying that they didn't. He could have 20 people praise him, but if one person criticized him—it would ruin his whole day. Many people liked John. But he had a *love him* or *hate him* personality. He had days when he wasn't easy to get along with. He was criticized if he didn't always say "please" and "thank you." Other days he was gregarious, and it was hard not to like him—unless your biases were set in stone. He was about to learn that these ups and downs are (and always have been) part of his biochemical nature.

John was not unlike other doctors. He wasn't perfect, but he did want to help people. And there probably never has been a doctor who didn't want their patients to do well … What possible reason could they have to not want good patient outcomes? But when there are bad outcomes, natural or otherwise, many people in our society want to have someone to blame. And they say doctors don't know how to communicate sympathy without seeming to admit negligence. Sometimes John wouldn't say anything—and then he'd be accused of callousness. Fortunately, John had some patients who taught him about life, communication, and dying with dignity. When Mike came in, for example, he taught Doctor John a few things he hadn't learned in medical school:

"How's it going today, Mike?" Doctor John was tentative about even asking the question, for he knew Mike had little reason to ever have a good day.

"I feel fine, Doc" Mike would respond, but John knew he was lying. "How's it going with you?"

The conversation would continue:

"Mike, you're an incredible man. You've had cancer, three heart attacks, a stroke, and heart failure. Yet you still come in here, month after month, and tell me you feel fine."

"Well, there's no point in complaining. I try to make the best of the situation."

Mike truly was an amazing man. The fact that he was still alive was a miracle. John suspected that it was his family support, faith in God, and positive attitude that had allowed him to live ten years longer than he was supposed to.

"Well, keep doing what you're doing then, Mike. I don't want to rock the boat," Doctor John would say. Patient Mike was *a bit crazy* to think everything was fine, but it was a good crazy. Too bad everyone can't be crazy that way.

(When Mike later died, Doctor John felt as bad as anyone in the family. He hugged Mike's family members, cried with them, and shared pleasant stories of how Mike used to be. He loved the story of how Mike met his wife: he eyed her from the balcony in church, followed her home one Sunday, and offered her a ride in his pickup truck. The wind was blowing that day. Hearing that his wife-to-be was having trouble keeping her skirt from blowing up made the story come to life. Right up to the day he died, Mike would look at his bride as if she was still a teenager. And she would look lovingly back at him, saddened by the realization that their 50 year romance was coming to an end.)

John's next patient, Nancy, wasn't lucky enough to have a physical sickness. She seemed to be in good health, but always felt terrible. Last month she had an imagined heart attack. Last week she had a "lump in her throat," and John was not able to find anything wrong. Her latest complaint was that she "couldn't walk"—but John had seen her walk normally from the parking lot through his office window.

"My legs are weak. What is it, Doctor?" she asked nervously. "Have I had a stroke? Or could it be a brain tumor? How do you know it's not a brain tumor? Or maybe it's Multiple Sclerosis? I know someone with MS, and it started out with weakness. What is it, Doctor? What's wrong with me?"

John hesitated to respond. "Let me do an exam first, Nancy. Let me see if I can figure it out." He carefully examined her from head to toe. He noticed that she deftly pulled her "weak" leg to the side when he dropped it: a reliable sign of hysteria. Her crossed leg test and reflexes were also normal.

"Well, Doctor, what is it?"

"It is a typical case of *transitory cerebral paresis*. I see it all the time. It can be due to a virus, sleep deprivation, and/or stress. It goes away in few days." He was stretching the truth, of course, but the *little white lie* was for her benefit. Pseudo-explanations and reassuring predictions are more of a treatment than a diagnosis. They're better than telling the patient their malady is in their head.

True to form, Nancy's mysterious leg weakness spontaneously resolved in less than two days. She returned to her usual state of chronic somatization, however. She isn't lying. She really does suffer from a variety of physical and mental discomfort. Anti-anxiety and antidepressant drugs have been tried, but she doesn't ever get a whole lot better—or any worse, for that matter. She might never change. These traits are biologically-based. Her personality is wrapped around her biology. She has another appointment scheduled for next month, and she'll probably have another illness by then. You see: Nancy is also *kinda' crazy*, but not a lethal kind of crazy.

When John was a young doctor he had the privilege of working with a famous and highly regarded psychiatrist. This psychiatrist had so many patients that he had to start his hospital rounds at 5 a.m. He would walk into a patient's room, turn on the lights, roust them from their sleep, and ask:

"Mr. Jones, how are you doing today?"

Mr. Jones was a paranoid schizophrenic. He had conversations with God. Sometimes he thought he had special powers. He spent most of his day afraid that evil forces (the devil, the charge nurse, and the neighbor lady) were plotting against him.

"I feel okay today, Doctor; but yesterday wasn't so good. And what's going to happen tomorrow? And when am I going to get out of here?"

"Stay in today!" the brilliant psychiatrist said. "If you keep one foot in yesterday, and the other foot in tomorrow, you'll crap on today."

"That makes sense," responded Mr. Jones.

The psychiatrist starting walking out of the room, but was interrupted by Mr. Jones.

"Doc, wait! I need to know something. I'm in this psychiatric ward. Does that mean—that you think I'm crazy? And when do I get to go home?"

The famous psychiatrist turned, thought for a moment, and responded:

My theory on crazy, Mr. Jones, *is that everybody is a little*—some more and some less. You're just crazier than other people. Since you're starting to realize this, you'll be able to go home soon."

"Thank you … I think," said Mr. Jones. But the doctor was gone, had entered another room, and was waking up another patient to see how their day was going.

Doctor John was now Patient John. It was a difficult transition. He agreed to see the psychiatrist with his wife. He hoped that he would be able to take a pill and make everything fine. John secretly wondered if he was crazy. But his crazy seemed different. His dad died from a medical mistake, and he wanted to make sure that never happened to any of his patients. And so he gets irritated by even little mistakes. Then he told the psychiatrist about a conversation he had with a nurse about a medication error:

"Nurse, don't you realize how dangerous it is to give that drug incorrectly?" Doctor John asked her.

The nurse responded something like this: "The night nurse gave the medicine before she left. I didn't know if it was given, so I gave the medicine myself. It was an honest mistake."

"Twice as much medicine as I prescribed can be dangerous. I hope the patient doesn't get heart or kidney problems from the mistake … And if something bad does happen—I'll be the one to get sued, not you."

"You shouldn't order that medicine if it's that dangerous," she said.

"It's not dangerous if you give it correctly," John said. "Besides, I want the patient to get better, and he needs the medicine.…" Doctor John pulled at his hair wondering how he could make his point without being labeled a jerk.

John had more encounters like this than he could count. He felt like he could never say the right thing to some people. They would find fault with whatever he said or did. And then one day he got into a shouting match with several nurses. They were upset with his telephone manners. He yelled at a nurse who was yelling at him. It is a matter of public record. Several days after the yelling episode, she filed an assault charge against him. She was intimated, she said. She also accused him of rubbing his belly against her chest, but (not surprisingly) nobody could substantiate that charge. The assault charge was dropped, but not before a one-sided account of allegations against him appeared in the newspaper. The same parties filed a complaint against him to the State Medical Board. They said his license should be suspended "in order to insure the public safety." The complaint was later dismissed. It took eight months and most of his savings to defend himself against these charges. There are rumors that he would also be sued. This has not yet happened; but that doesn't help him sleep at night.

"Of course I'm afraid," John told the psychiatrist. "It's not paranoia if the threats are real."

John would obsess about these matters for days. He no longer knew what was real and what was imagined. He used to work in a tireless manner, but lately didn't have any energy. He had more down days than up. He wanted to feel better. He didn't want people to hate him. He knew there was something wrong. That's why he had been willing to see the psychiatrist with his wife.

"John," the psychiatrist said, *"you're not a bad person.* Sometimes you have behavior that annoys people, though. Everybody has bad days; but you also have a disease that can make disagreements escalate out of control. Believe it or not, this can be both a blessing and a curse. You have *Bipolar Disorder*, also called Manic-Depressive Illness; and you've probably had it all your life."

"Doc, does that mean I'm crazy?" John asked.

The psychiatrist thought for a moment, and then responded, "John, *my theory on crazy* is that *everybody is a little*—some more and some less. Your disease means you are just *a little crazier* than other people."

"Having a mental illness," the psychiatrist continued, "isn't the worst thing in the world. Bipolar Disorder affects one out of fifty people. Many productive people have had the disorder: Christopher Columbus, Abraham Lincoln, Dale Carnegie,

Sylvia Plath, Patty Duke, Buzz Aldrin, Charlie Pride, John Daly, and Jim Carrey.

"Medication will help," he said. "You'll also need to make some changes in how you live. This is not a terminal disease—even though you might think it is. Calm down. Avoid stress."

The meeting with the psychiatrist had gone fairly well. John and his wife liked him and respected him. What he said made sense. John was disappointed that he had a *mental illness*, though. He knew there was a stigma with such a diagnosis. John was grateful his wife had stood by him through the years.

"Grace," he said to his wife, "what would I do without you? I'm sorry for ever yelling at you. I know how difficult I can be to live with. Thank God for putting you in my life."

"That's nice of you to say," Grace responded. "And I'm sorry for yelling at you. Sometimes you're even fun to be around. I don't want to shock you, but I also have faults. I shouldn't admit it, but—*I'm a little crazy too.*"

"What?" John asked. "You mean you're crazy like me?"

"Not like you … Nobody's *that* crazy," she said with a grin. "I'm crazy in my own way."

Grace smiled at John. He smiled back. She snuggled up to him, took his hand, and they walked away from the clinic, together, not knowing what would happen next.

"I take you ... to have and to hold from this day forward, for better or worse, for richer for poorer, in sickness and in health, to love and to cherish, till death do us part."

Traditional Wedding Vows, Book of Common Prayer.

Thoughts on Crazy:

"There was only one catch and that was Catch-22, which specified that a concern for one's safety in the face of dangers that were real and immediate was the process of a rational mind. Orr [a war pilot] was crazy and could be grounded. All he had to do was ask; and as soon as he did, he would no longer be crazy and would have to [go back into battle] … If he [fought] … he was crazy and didn't have to; but if he didn't want to he was sane and had to … That's the catch, that Catch-22"

Joseph Heller, C.1961, <u>Catch-22</u>,
Dell Publishing Co, Inc, p 47.

"Man is certainly crazy. He could not make a mite, and [yet] he makes gods by the dozen."

Montaigne, 3rd century Greek philosopher.

"Going Stir Crazy"
"That Crazy Fool"
"Crazy in Love"
"Crazy like a Fox"

Common Crazy Metaphors.

11. Naked

Occasionally John would sit in church (and other public gatherings) and take a mental inventory of how many people were his patients. The number was rather impressive. This is a small town, he realized; and there weren't that many primary care doctors to choose from. John had seen over half of the people that lived here. Some of these people had seen him for minor problems only, but many had been his *regular patients*: people he did yearly exams on, took care of their chronic problems, and managed all their medical needs.

Most people hate going to the doctor for their yearly exams. They hate getting poked and prodded. They hate having anyone know if they are skinny or fat. They hate having anyone know if they have abused or misused their physical bodies. They hate—to put it bluntly—to be seen naked.

And now the shoe was on the other foot … Doctor John Smith was publicly accused of inappropriate behavior. The newspapers said he not only yelled at a nurse, but he (somehow) rubbed his belly against her chest. John felt his reputation was tarnished no matter how the case turned out. When John's doctor told him to quit, he took him up on the offer. The experience of being a small town doctor didn't seem to be worth it anymore. It had been like living in a fishbowl. He was tired of being a target for every Dawn, Mick, and Carrie who might want to criticize him. He couldn't afford to defend himself against any more ridiculous charges. He felt stripped of his defenses. He felt naked.

In years gone by, John's family was proud of him and his standing in the community. Now the tables are turned. Now John was merely a homemaker. They were the ones who had to do battle with the world. John was very proud of his family, but he was afraid they were no longer proud of him. When they came home from work or school, they wonder what he did all day. Never mind that he did household chores—did he get anything done?

Doctor John was now just a house husband. He enjoyed what he did. He was good at it. It's too bad his wife and kids don't understand his work, though. He gets up early, makes coffee, and has just a few minutes to myself. After that, it's go, go, go! He struggles to get the kids up and off to school. He makes the meals and cleans the kitchen. He picks up the clothes they have thrown around the house. He does the laundry. He sorts through the junk mail. He pays the bills on time. He cleans the toilet and washes windows. He keeps up the yard. And he always has a special project. One day he paints the fence. On another day he organizes the junk drawer. His days are always busy.

John knows many people don't think much of the work he now does. But he knows his contribution to society is significant. Although some people think it is trite, he knows the saying is true: "A man's work is never done!" And so it is. John's family, friends, and acquaintances don't appreciate him anymore. They don't like what the man of the house has become.

John is learning how to live with this lack of respect. He has started to exercise again. He is trying to lose his midriff bulge. He is trying to pick out his clothes better—so he doesn't look so dowdy. He tries to stay up on the news. He even reads books. He doesn't want to sound stupid when people talk to him. He is trying to improve himself. He is trying to be the best house husband he can be.

"Be who you are and say what you feel, because those who mind don't matter and those who matter don't mind."

Dr. Seuss, Author and Illustrator, 1991, www.quotationspage.com

12. For Men Only

Have you ever wondered why women are the way they are? Despite what feminists say, there are very significant differences between men and women. These differences start either in the womb or in the Garden of Eden, depending on your religious persuasion, and the result is that the opposite sexes have—duh, *opposite* ways of interacting with the world. Sure there are little girls that are good at math, and there are even little boys who like to play with dolls, but these are the exceptions. Have you known any women that could have played on your high school football team? I suspect you have. Some women are strong as oxen. And some women cuss more than sailors. Likewise, there are men who are indisputably *pretty*. I know you don't want to admit it, but some men are prettier than any of the women you've ever gone out with. But I'm not talking about cross-dressing, homosexuality androgyny, or embryology here. I'm talking about middle-America *Mom and Pop* people. Men and women use a toilet in different ways, so their psychosocial differences must also be significant.

Gender, genetic, and environmental variation make this world an interesting place. Women are different from men: not in all things, of course, but often enough to make this important in our day to day lives. Can we, as men, put this information to good use? I hope so; otherwise I wouldn't bother to write this. We need to know something about the opposite sex. I'm not a woman, so many would dismiss my opinions as invalid. But who else can you ask? A woman certainly isn't going to divulge her secrets, even if she is aware of them. Besides, I've been around women all my life: my mother is a woman; I have six sisters; I've been married 24 years; and I've worked around women all my life. I am, for all intents and purposes, an *expert* on women—from a man's perspective, that is.

The experts say men think about sex *way* more often than women do. We could debate this point, and other known facts of anatomy and physiology, but I would rather not … You probably learned everything you need to know about sex in middle school, anyway. But were you paying attention? Remember when all the girls were taller than you? They weren't just trying to embarrass you. Your female classmates were acquiring breasts, pubic hair, and child-rearing capacity. It might have taken you several years to notice, but they were becoming women. You were, of course, worried about your acne, social inadequacies, and body odor. They were interested in relationships. They wanted to go out on dates. Chances are that you "didn't understand" what was going on, so most of your female classmates dated older guys.

Of course you didn't know what was going on! You were—and probably still are—just your average dumb guy! *Take it easy, buddy.* I'm on your side. We're all dumb guys, to some extent. For some of us, it's been all down hill since puberty. We just get dumber and dumber, relatively speaking, to the women in our lives. Those of you with daughters already know this fact. For those of you that are married, your wives may be hiding this information from you. Why else, do you suppose, did they marry an older guy—*I'm talking about you!*—have you buy life insurance, and want to go out to eat all the time? Did your wife ever ask you to work out at the gym? Wake up and smell the coffee. She isn't really "the weaker sex." Among other things, she is going to outlive you. Why do you think she collects all those travel brochures?

It is possible to wise up to these realities of life. You can live out the remaining years of your life in ignorant bliss, if that's what it is; or you can learn what it takes to co-exist with the women in your life. You might be dumb but you're not stupid, you know. Men consistently score better than women on college entrance exams. (Be careful, though; *someone* is changing the format of these tests so that women can outperform men.) Men are better at analyzing things. Men aren't as easily distracted as women are. Men are physically stronger than women. But all this doesn't matter if we don't recognize areas of life where women are more gifted than us: they integrate facts and feelings better; they get along better with others; and they have a secret power—it's called intuition. They don't care how a telephone works. All they care about is whether or not they can call their sister. They don't need to have a goal for all of their activities. They can carry on a conversation just for the fun of it. Keep this in mind the next time your wife wants to converse. Don't focus on what's being said—just pretend to listen, nod in agreement, and occasionally say: "Yes, dear."

Visiting with others without a need to manipulate or control is *sociable*. Women are definitely better than men in this regard. You're not a sissy if you master this art. In a similar way, brushing your teeth, combing your hair, applying deodorant, and occasionally using cologne won't kill you— and might make it easier for you to mingle. I don't always do these things. And smelling bad really isn't cool. When people turn up their nose to me, they are (I presume) just trying to preserve their olfactory nerve. And most people instinctively avoid other people and situations that don't smell right. Likewise, walking away from someone who isn't acting civilized is a matter of survival. If we want to do well in this civilized world, then we men should all try to smell good and act civilized.

Saying please and thank you is useful. Grunting your wants and needs might have worked in caveman days, but is positively anachronistic nowadays. Knowledge of the English language is also useful. And call people by their name. Dale Carnegie, in his book <u>How to Win Friends & Influence People</u>, says a person's name is "music to their ears." How do you feel if someone forgets your name? See what I mean? It doesn't win any friends if you call them by the wrong name, so at least pretend you remember in your forgetful moments. Knowing how to talk is one thing—but sometimes saying nothing is better than putting your foot in your mouth.

Women instinctively know these things. While prehistoric man was out hunting, his female counterpart was gathering crops, making coffee, and borrowing a cup of sugar from the neighbor. We may be good at killing things; but that ability doesn't help us in modern times. We have to unlearn these primitive aggressive tendencies. Women have lots of attributes that we men should emulate. Take the best of their world and integrate it into our world of watching football, golfing, and other activities that you certainly don't need to give up. As to the social graces, you can "fake it 'til you make it." You can pretend to be nice even if you aren't. We need to be interdependent with our neighbors if we want to get that cup of sugar, piece of pie, invitation to dinner, and fellowship of friends—things the female of our species have known for centuries.

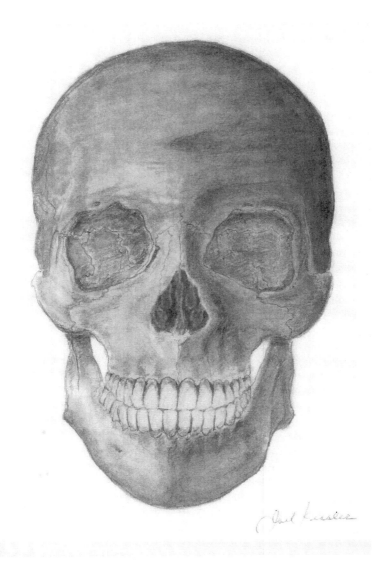

"Physician, heal thyself." Bible, Luke 4:23, KJV

(Drawing by Joel A. Kessler, 2006)

13. Broken

Our Health Care System is sick, and in need of Intensive Care. Health Care costs have risen from 6% to 16% of the Gross National Product in the last 50 years. We spend about $5000 per person per year on Health Care—which is twice that of other industrialized nations. And according to the Commonwealth Fund report released 9/20/06 (as reported in the US News & World Report), the United States system gets low grades on outcomes, quality of care, access to care, and efficiency—compared to other industrialized nations or generally accepted standards of care.

The USA ranks at the bottom among industrialized countries for life expectancy both at birth and at age 60. It is also last on infant mortality, with 7 deaths per 1,000 live births, compared with 2.7 in the top three countries. Too many people can't afford to get preventive services, and subsequently get sicker before they come to medical attention—and require costlier care in the long run. Too many people smoke cigarettes, are obese, and aren't taking care of themselves. Too many people ignore their health—and yet expect doctors and hospitals to fix them when something goes wrong.

The system is broken. The money incentive isn't working anymore. Doctors, patients, and lawmakers apparently don't know the cost of these activities, so many unnecessary tests are ordered. An estimated $300 billion is spent per year in this country on defensive medicine practices. And $50 to 100 billion is wasted per year on paperwork. As a share of total health expenditures, insurance administrative costs in the USA are more than three times the rate of countries with integrated payment systems. We have about 46 million people in our country without health insurance. Our pharmaceutical companies come up with many innovations, but many people can't afford their products. And we do more elective surgery than any country in the world. There are 1.3 million abortions done in the USA per year. Twice as many hysterectomies are done here than in Europe. (Fibroids, for example, usually shrink as women get older; so conservative treatment may be all that is needed.) And colonoscopy, a test for colon cancer, is cost-effective if done for the recommended amount of $800 (for doctor & hospital)—but costs $3000 in some areas.

Every facet of our Health Care System will claim that they are doing their job—and it's the other guy who is at fault. The truth is: every person and every department must share responsibility for our failing Health Care System. Litigation reform is essential. Since Congress contains a preponderance of lawyers, however, they're not about to bite the hand that feeds them. Patients should take better care of themselves. They should be better informed consumers. Doctors should spend more time with patients, get to know them, and decipher what is really needed—instead of just ordering another CT scan or prescribing another medicine. The various Health Care professionals need to work better together. There is way too much jealousy, infighting, and back-stabbing. Everyone wants a bigger piece of the pie, of course. If these "professionals" don't learn to cooperate there won't be anything left for any of them. If there isn't improvement, then much of your local Health Care may one day be provided by Walmart-style operators in distant cities.

Thoughts on Our Legalistic Society:

"Did you know that you [all people, not just doctors] have a 1 in 4 chance of having a potentially devastating lawsuit filed against you sometime in the future? There are currently 80 to 90 million lawsuits filed in this country each year. That is over 150 suits per minute! [With less than 5% of the world's population, the USA has] over 70% of the world's lawyers … and we are adding new ones at a rate of 50,000 per year! What do you think those new lawyers are going to do to the number of lawsuits filed annually?"

by Jim Williams, "Protect Yourself From Our Litigious Society," 2003, from <u>Money Matters</u>, 4hb.com.

"The scent of these armpits aroma finer than prayer"

Walt Whitman, "Song of Myself," from Leaves of Grass, 1965, Airmont Publishing Co, pg 54.

"There's no such thing as a bad job."

Jerome A. Kessler, 2005.

14. Another Job

John Smith showed up for his new job at 6 a.m. It was still dark. He was right on time, as usual. Although he was *retired*, he was always willing to work. He was to be a truck driver for "Lucky Seven Farms" during the upcoming sugar beet harvest. It was a chance to make a little spending money. He also wanted to be part of the harvest frenzy.

"Thanks for coming," said Mr. Panko, head of the family farm cooperation. "You'll be working with my son, Jim. I think he wants you to drive the red truck. You'll have to check with him on that. He'll be your boss this year."

Another job. Another boss. It was all the same to John. He's had so many jobs in his life—he couldn't remember them all.

"Get in the red truck, John" said Jim Panko. "We just got these trucks last year, so please take care of them. And remember, with the nine speeds on these Kenworth trucks, you never ever use the clutch ... unless you have to."

It was, indeed, important to be good to the farmer's trucks. They were the lifeblood of the farming operation: they brought the crop to market, and were a necessary link in the farmer's ability to transform months of work into a paycheck.

The four beet trucks pulled out of the yard in single file. They went in darkness to a beet field where a defoliator was taking the leaves off the beets. This machine was followed by another machine that dug the beets, rolled them halfway up the ferris-wheel conveyor, put them in a storage bin, and then transferred the beets out on another conveyor belt to the waiting trucks. The beet trucks drove closely alongside the beet digger to receive the beets. When the truck was loaded, it drove to the beet dump, and another truck pulled up next to the digger. The process was repeated over and over again. The object was to keep the beet digger as busy as possible. It took four trucks in rotation to keep up with the farmer and his beet digger.

Working 12 hours per day, John could haul 8 loads of beets per day, and 20 tons of beets per load. That means that the beets John hauled during harvest contributed to the production of over 6 million pounds of sugar per year. That was enough to make two million gallons of Kool-Aid ®, seven thousand boxes of frosted flakes, *and* eleven thousand candy bars. He felt good about the contribution he was making to society. He was making a lot of kids happy—and hyperactive.

The beet trucks take their load to a huge sugar beet dumpsite. Each truck has to carefully dump its load through a steel trap door, where the beets are moved by conveyor belts, and then stacked by a huge beet piler. Dozens of trucks wait in line for their turn to dump beets. It is a hectic process; and anything that slows things down can be irritating. Workers at the beet dump get mad if truckers spill any beets. Although John hauls millions and millions of beets each harvest, he hates spilling even one. He knows that each and every beet has value. And spilled beets are messy. Much to John's chagrin, he did spill a few beets … And the piler operator cussed at him for it. She was an impatient woman. She told John to empty his load faster and quicker. John felt terrible that he caused the piler assistants extra work: whenever any beets were spilled, they had to pick them up. It was the worst part of their job. After spilling beets a second time, John felt especially bad.

A Mexican piler assistant, a middle-aged man who was missing several front teeth, came up to him, and asked:

"Is this a Kenworth truck?"

"Yes," John responded.

"I thought so," he said. "These trucks suck! They have a steel plate in back that keeps you from backing up close enough to the trapdoor, so you spill beets if you lift your box too fast …" That was the answer! Fred was relieved to find out there was a reason for his spillage. Out of the mouth of a laborer came the words of wisdom he was looking for. Now all he had to do was avoid bossy piler operators: ones who didn't realize he had to take his time. John hardly spilled any beets after that. He could once again take pride in his work.

John tried to do his best in all his jobs. Rumor is that he once had a really good job, but nobody knows what it was. That was many years ago. In recent years he has had a variety of physical labor jobs. He has cleaned toilets, planted trees, and drove truck. He really enjoys driving truck. Whatever he does he always tries to do his best. He is a hard worker. He is an example of that old-fashioned American work ethic: *Honest wages for an honest day's work* … He believed the saying was true. He does like getting paid, but probably would even work for free—just so he could go home at night with the knowledge that he's done a good job.

John is still married. He and his wife, Grace, have three sons. The boys are all grown up and moved away. They rarely came back to visit anymore. His wife developed Alzheimer's disease at a young age. She needs a lot of care. He kept her at home as long as he could. Last year John had to move her to the nursing home. Now he lives alone.

John dated quite a few girls in his youth. A few people have told him that his wife really isn't alive anymore—with her severe Alzheimer's disease—and he should get divorced. He should get back into the dating world.

"You're still a relatively young man," a friend said. "You need to get on with your life."

John didn't say anything. He thought about how it used to be. He used to be handsome, but now isn't particularly attractive. He eats too much junk food. He doesn't pay much attention to his looks. John can't really picture himself back in the dating world. And he wouldn't even know what to say in a woman's company.

An attractive older woman recently approached John. She seemed to have more than a casual interest in him. She asked: "How have you been lately? Tell me about yourself ..."

"There's not much to tell," John responded.

"You must still have hopes and fears, don't you? Do you get lonely? I know I do," she said. He didn't take the hint. He said nothing. She went on: "Well ... say something!"

"What's there to say? I like to work," John said. "Even though my wife doesn't talk—since her Alzheimer's got so bad—I still visit her every day at the nursing home."

"That sounds depressing," she said.

John described his wife in unrealistic terms. Even though she couldn't talk, he visited with her everyday. She couldn't feed or dress herself. She couldn't control her bladder or bowels. She once had many friends. She helped people celebrate every occasion. She helped people deal with their losses. He described her as a person that people are still attracted to. She had been the center of his life—and still is.

"She's had a fever lately. I think it's getting better. Her appetite hasn't been very good. It takes a long time to feed her, so I've been spending more time at *the home* lately. But I need to keep busy. So I work a lot of temporary jobs. I like to work. Any kind of work will do. There's no such thing as a bad job. You never should be ashamed of what kind of work you do."

John's conversations would revolve around whatever work he was doing. He didn't know what else to talk about. As time went on, John didn't mind that he didn't really have any social life. He just spent more and more of his free time with his wife at the nursing home. He just sat there. He talked to her, but there was never a response. And he still works whenever he can. He enjoys his work. He enjoys his life. He just hopes that he can find another job when beet harvest is over.

Thoughts on Appearance:

"Because you are greasy or pimpled, or were once drunk, or a thief, Or that you are diseas'd, or rheumatic, or a prostitute, Or from frivolity or impotence, or that you are no scholar and never saw your name in print, Do you give in that you are any less immortal?"

by Walt Whitman, "A Song for Occupations," from Leaves of Grass, 1965, Airmont Publishing Co, pg 159.

"What advantage does a wise man have over someone who is foolish? What does a poor man gain by knowing how to act toward others? Being satisfied with what you have is better than always wanting more."

Bible, Ecclesiastes 6:8-9, NIRV.

"Whoever exalts himself shall be humbled; and whoever humbles himself shall be exalted."

Bible, Matthew 23:12, NASB.

"Charm is deceptive, and beauty is fleeting; but a woman who fears the Lord is to be praised."

Bible, Proverbs 31:30, NIV.

"Then adorn yourself with glory and splendor, and clothe yourself in honor and majesty."

Bible, Job 40:10, NIV.

15. Promise to Mom

Dad is gone now, and Mom is sick, but I remember how it was when they were healthy. Before the Thanksgiving table was even cleaned, Mom would get the whole family in gear for Christmas decorating. We would have at least three decorated Christmas trees in the house. Two would be artificial, but we'd always get a real tree for the living room.

"They don't have any good trees in Twin Junction," she'd say. Back then our family lived in Twin Junction. Barnsville, another small town, was located just 50 miles away. Both towns offered about the same services, but some people always thought *the other town* had more to offer than *their town*.

"Drive over to Barnsville to get a *nice* Christmas tree," she'd tell Dad. "And don't come back with anything cheap! It has to be a skinny tree with short needles; and it has to be eight feet tall."

Dad would grumble a bit, and then dutifully drive to Barnsville to look for an acceptable tree. One year he brought home a tree that Grace didn't like. They had an argument. He reluctantly brought the long-needled tree, a Norway pine, back to the vendor. He was embarrassed by the ordeal. Dad liked to think he was the man of the house, and his word goes. Everybody knew Mom always got her way, though—at least on subjects like Christmas, house decorations, and color of clothes. Dad's brief protest was usually followed by the later admission that Mom's choice was better. He liked how the house looked after Mom was done with her Christmas decorating. More importantly, he enjoyed how Mom transformed our house into everybody's favorite place to gather for the holidays. He was proud of the house. He was proud of his wife and his family. He knew she was the force that made Christmas a joyous time of the year.

As the middle of three sons, I had a unique perspective as to what makes a family click. Our house always had something going on. Dad was a doctor. Mom was a nurse. We always had heated conversations on a variety of subjects. Sometimes Mom and Dad got into arguments, but they always found a way to resolve their differences. Then they'd act like newlyweds again—at least until the next credit card statement (or other item of dissension) got them into another argument. We boys always had a variety of activities to keep us busy: school, sports, friends, civic clubs, etc. We kept our parents busy driving us from place to place. After we learned to drive, we all started going our own way. That was the beginning of our transition into adults. Mom and Dad had to get to know each other all over again. It was an interesting change of events; and I enjoyed watching the drama of our lives unfold.

Mom always said we got our brains from Dad, but our personality from her. Dad didn't mind that analysis, and admitted that he married Mom because she was wholesome—and softened the hardness of his own character. Mom always said I was a blend of their two personalities.

It was interesting to see how my parents interacted with each other, and with us kids. That early experience no doubt influenced my later decision to become a psychologist. I now work as a family counselor in a Midwestern city. My practice is affiliated with a medical clinic, so I frequently consult on the care of families with medical problems.

One "family situation" I learned from was watching how my parents resolved their differences. As I recall, Mom didn't think much of Dad's fashion sense. That's why she didn't trust his choice in Christmas trees, and she was very specific in the kind of tree she wanted.

"Did you see that awful tree Dad brought home?" she whispered to me. "Your dad might be smart, but he doesn't know a thing about decorating." Mom didn't think Dad could even dress himself. He would wear an orange shirt with blue pants, and think it looked just fine. Eventually Dad learned to accept Mom's advice on what he should wear. He learned it was just easier to submit to her preferences on wallpaper, furniture, and paint colors. Mom refused to lose arguments on matters of clothing and decorations. She loved teasing Dad on his lack of fashion sense.

"Boys," she would say at the dinner table, "when I get Alzheimer's disease, and go to the nursing home, don't let your dad pick out my clothes. Promise me that you will make sure that my clothes match. I wouldn't be able to stand it if I was put in a pink polka dot blouse and green-striped pants." We all laughed—even Dad. Mom smiled when she said this, but seemed genuinely concerned that she wouldn't look good in her old age. She could live with the prospect of being confused, but not with the idea that her clothes wouldn't match.

One August evening (when I was 17), the family had a quiet gathering—complete with our favorite meal (spaghetti), a homemade cake, and a nice sense of togetherness. It was to be the last time we got together in this manner. My older brother was off to college the following day. My younger brother and I missed him, but were busy with our own lives. My parents got more and more sentimental when we got together for family meals. We were each developing separate lives. Our parents were getting old. A few years later, Dad had a heart attack, and couldn't work anymore. And just like Dad predicted, Mom got Alzheimer's disease. Dad kept her home as long as he could, but eventually had to put her into the local nursing home.

Dad visited Mom at the nursing home twice a day. He stopped by in the mid-morning to make sure her days were off to a good start. She had received her morning pills, been fed, and usually needed to be cleaned of food that had missed her mouth. The aides had already dressed her. Dad inspected their choice of clothes, and insisted she be changed if her clothes didn't match … Over the years Dad had learned what Mom liked, and some of Mom's fashion sense had rubbed off on him. Each afternoon he would visit again. He would watch TV, review the news with her, and converse with her as if she understood what he was talking about. The nursing home staff didn't always like having Dad around. Eventually they got used to how critical he was to their choice of her clothes. They came to appreciate his visits. While he was there, she was one less resident that they had to worry about.

One day Dad didn't show up for his daily inspection of Mom's attire. The nursing home staff joked about it. When he didn't come in the afternoon, however, they wondered if he was all right. A neighbor was called. The house was entered. They found Dad dead in his reading chair. He appeared to have died peacefully while reading. One of his favorite books was found on the floor next to him.

After Dad died, I moved Mom to a nursing home in the city where I work. My wife and kids visited her whenever they could, but gradually tired of the routine. Mom hadn't been able to speak for years. She required assistance with all her activities. I visited her every day. I spent my lunch hours with her. As I fed her, I remembered how it was when my brothers and I came home for lunch when we were kids. Growing up in our small town, the schools were just a few blocks away; and it was always nice to go home for lunch and see Mom's smiling face as she fed us a sandwich, soup, and cookies. And now I am feeding her. The thought of how times had changed brought tears to my eyes ... I looked at the wrinkled brown slacks and white blouse she had on that day. There were bits of food and saliva on her shirt ... I realized that soon she would be gone. I vowed once again to keep the promise I had made to her. She had always been a wonderful mom. It was good to be with her even now, and I was grateful that her clothes still matched.

16. Journey's End

When I was a small boy, Dad and I started on a December trip to Fargo. Mom and my brothers were already there—staying with her family. Dad said we "just had to get there" before midnight. Dad heard that there was a shortcut that would save time, so he took the unfamiliar road hoping to reduce our travel time. The weather forecast said there would be snow. We were getting a late start, however; because we had to wait for Dad to be done with work and my school program to be over.

The turn wasn't well marked. We turned south, as advised, but soon the road was a winding road through the badlands of western North Dakota. There weren't any other cars on that road. The compass on our vehicle occasionally said *south*—our intended direction—but just as often said every other direction. Because it was dark, we couldn't tell if we were making progress or not.

The road turned from asphalt to gravel. We passed over a cattle gate. The silhouette of livestock could occasionally be seen. We occasionally saw a few buildings, but none of them had any lights on. It would have been nice to have someone to help us with directions, but we didn't see any people in the area. There wasn't any cell phone coverage either. When we started the trip, Dad and I were talking cheerfully. Now we were silent. Even though I was just a young boy, I knew Dad was worried. Something was wrong. And certainly the road and the weather could get us into trouble.

"Dad," I asked, "when are we going to get there?"

"I don't know. I must have taken the wrong turn. I'm afraid we're lost."

I looked at him with disbelief. I think it was the first time I realized that adults can make mistakes. It was particularly eerie to hear my dad admit he didn't know where he was going. I was afraid. I didn't want Dad to think I was a baby, so I tried not to cry.

"Dad, what's wrong?" I asked. "Can't we just go home?"

I was mad that Mom and Dad had taken separate paths for our holiday vacation. They should have stayed together. We all should have stayed together. It was stupid to think we always had to travel for Christmas. I wanted to know where we were, and when we would get to our destination.

A light snow was becoming much thicker now. Dad was having a hard time keeping the windshield clean. It was hard to see. The low visibility and winding road was a recipe for disaster. Our vehicle could easily slip off the road. We were in the middle of nowhere. We could be stranded and freeze to death. I *just knew* Dad had the same fear.

My two brothers were with Mom and her family in Fargo. That was a long way from our home; and they might not know for many hours if we were lost. Our frozen bodies could be eaten by wolves before anyone even knew we were missing. It was stupid to have gone on this trip. It was stupid for Dad to have taken this short-cut.

My thoughts wandered to what was really important in life. I always wanted way too many *things*: a video game, a new computer, another hockey stick, and chocolate pancakes at a local restaurant. No matter what I got, I always wanted *more.* Mom and Dad made sure we always got what we *needed*; and they also usually gave us most of the things we *wanted*. I was too selfish, I realized; and promised to myself I would stop being that way.

"We're going to be okay," my dad said, trying to sound reassuring. "We'll soon come to a road I recognize. But—just in case—maybe we should say a prayer. Do you know any prayers?" my dad asked.

"Only one," I said. "It's the one we say with Mom every night."

"Well, let's say it. You start, and I'll try to follow."

"Dear God, I know that I have sinned. And You sent your son, Jesus, to die for my sins. I trust You now as my Savior. Thank You for forgiving me, and giving me life that lasts forever. Amen."

I said the words, and Dad followed along ... We paused after the prayer was completed. We both felt better. Despite the uncertainty about our condition, we were confident that everything would be okay. Dad drove slowly along—trying not to slip into the ditch. And soon we came to a fork in the road. Dad wasn't sure which way to turn. He turned right, and the compass said we were headed north. That was opposite of how we started. We no longer wanted to go to the big city.

It wasn't too long before we came to another promising road. There were a few cars on the road. We saw some lights in the distance. That road led to another decent road. Finally we got to a road we recognized as being the way home. Before we knew it, we were home again. We had been just a few hours from home when it seemed like we were completely lost. And our home never looked so good! We turned on all the lights, started a fire, and sat together in front of the fireplace. We called Mom, and told her about our adventure:

"We were lost, Mom … I taught Dad our prayer, and then we found our way." And Dad agreed with me. Our family prayer, taught to us by Mom, had calmed us and guided us home.

We stayed at home that Christmas. Dad and I talked and played games. I got to know Dad like never before. Mom and my brothers came home a few days later. Our family was happy to be reunited. Although we didn't do much that year, we had our best Christmas ever.

I learned that Christmas that we had been in too much of a hurry. Somewhere along the way we got lost. Getting there had become more important than the journey. And so it is now with my own life, and this book. If the journey isn't appreciated, then it doesn't matter where you're going.

978-0-595-42398-9
0-595-42398-1